The Three-Day Traffic Jam

JOHN KEEFAUVER

SIMON & SCHUSTER BOOKS FOR YOUNG READERS

Published by Simon & Schuster

New York • London • Toronto • Sydney • Tokyo • Singapore

SIMON & SCHUSTER BOOKS FOR YOUNG READERS
Simon & Schuster Building, Rockefeller Center
1230 Avenue of the Americas, New York, New York 10020

SIMON & SCHUSTER BOOKS FOR YOUNG READERS
is a trademark of Simon & Schuster.
Designed by Lucille Chomowicz
Manufactured in the United States of America   10 9 8 7 6 5 4 3 2 1
Library of Congress Cataloging-in-Publication Data
Keefauver, John. The three-day traffic jam / John Keefauver.
p. cm.
Summary: When he takes his father's precious new car out, eleven-year-old Henry causes a
traffic jam that is huge even by twenty-first century southern California standards.
[1. Traffic congestion—Fiction.   2. Fathers and sons—Fiction.
3. California—Fiction.]   I. Title.   II. Title: 3-day traffic jam.
PZ7.K22555Th   1992   [Fic]—dc20   91-30583 CIP
ISBN: 0-671-75599-4

To Margaret Kolodzie, who helped me out of more than one jam in the writing of this book

1

Little did I know that today I would cause a traffic jam that might last longer than the one in 1999. That one lasted eleven months and was two hundred miles long and eighty miles wide. This one might be even bigger. What makes it even worse is that I was driving Dad's car when I caused the jam. I shouldn't have been driving it for two reasons: He hadn't given me permission, and I'm eleven years old.

What happened was that Dad bought this big, fancy car and went crazy over it. He bragged about its speed, power, price, steering, thirty coats of paint, computerized engine, and anything else he could think of. He got a big thrill out of just sitting in it in the driveway.

Then he'd get out of it and gently rub it down—for hours—with the softest cloth he could buy.

He not only talked about the car, he talked to it. "How's my Sweetie Pie today?" he'd say. *Ugh!* "Want to take a little ride, Sweetie?" Double *ugh*! He talked to it more than he did to me. I could be invisible as far as he was concerned. If I got in it, I had to take off my shoes first. It's a wonder he even let me get in it. And he wouldn't let me in it by myself. I think he was afraid I'd stick my tongue out at it and hurt its feelings. And I probably would have. I didn't even begin to think about asking him if I could drive it.

He'd taught me to drive his old 1997 clunker, which he still had. It was parked behind the garage he kept Sweetie Pie locked up in. Not that I drove the clunker on the freeways and expressways. I just drove it on our property. We live on about half an acre of land that doesn't have pavement on it yet, except for the driveway. Our yard is covered with grass, which is unusual these days. Dad told me that when he was a kid there were a lot more places that didn't have pavement. Not now. When I

look out from our house, all I see are freeways
and expressways. Our house is right next to
them. Right *in* them, actually. We live in Los
Angeles.

Anyway, Dad had fallen in love with Sweetie
Pie. It was almost as if it came first and I came
second. I didn't like that at all, especially since
only Dad and I were living at home now. Mom
and Dad split not too long ago, and I just see her
once in a while. The divorce was tough on Dad.
Mom was the one who wanted it. He bought
Sweetie Pie right after Mom moved out.

So anyway, a few days before July Fourth I
thought it would be great if Dad and I and
Tillie-Jean went to see the fireworks on the
Fourth. They would be at Redondo Beach,
which is on the Pacific Ocean and not too far
from our house. Tillie-Jean is a girl about my
age who was coming to visit us July third for a
couple of weeks or so. She is the daughter of
people Dad and Mom knew, and she had visited
us before with her folks. This time she was coming by herself while her mom and dad went to
Europe.

When I asked Dad if we could go to the fireworks, he said, "No chance. There will be too

much holiday traffic for Sweetie Pie. She might get smashed up."

I halfway expected him to say that. He was afraid to drive Sweetie Pie in almost any traffic. It just sat in the driveway or garage most of the time getting loved.

"So let's go in the clunker," I said.

"It needs work. I don't trust it the way it is."

I didn't either, but I'd be willing to chance it. Actually, we didn't use either car often. Dad went to work in a helicopter pool, and I went to school in a school bus.

"Besides, Joe Saunders is picking me up the afternoon of the Fourth," Dad went on. "An auto parts place is having a holiday sale on new computer terminals for cars." His voice began to get excited, something that happened every time he started talking about cars lately. "These new terminals will give navigation information to a driver by utilizing communication satellites. Want to go?"

"Nah."

"I'll be home in time for us to watch the fireworks on TV."

"In Sweetie Pie?" I was being sarcastic. He was forever watching television on the car's set, because he claimed it had better reception than any of the sets in the house.

He knew I was being sarcastic. "Maybe—but not in those clothes you have on now. They're filthy."

I was mad. And by the Fourth I was madder. I felt like setting off a giant firecracker inside Sweetie Pie. And I could have actually done it. Because after Dad left with Joe Saunders, I saw the keys to both the garage and Sweetie Pie lying in the bathroom, where Dad had dressed after a shower. I stuck them in my pocket.

They were still in my pocket later on in the afternoon when Tillie-Jean came out on the porch where I was sitting, still mad. "What's the matter, Henry?" she asked.

I grunted.

"Are you mad at me?"

I shook my head. I liked her okay, for a girl.

"Has your dad left?"

"Yeah. He'll probably come home bragging about some new computer he's bought for Sweetie Pie."

She gave me a long look. "You sure don't like that car, do you?"

I gave her another grunt.

She stared at me, as if she were thinking about something. Then she said, "Has your dad let you drive it yet?"

She had just come to start her visit the evening before, and we hadn't talked about much yet. But she heard Dad bragging about Sweetie Pie plenty, and I guessed she'd seen how I reacted to all his bragging. One thing I knew, she'd been very impressed when I'd taken her for a drive in the old clunker the last time she'd been here, a few months ago. Mom and Dad had just split. And she wanted me to take her for a ride in Sweetie Pie, too, which Dad had just bought. That was one of the reasons I wanted to learn to drive Sweetie Pie. It had been great driving the clunker with somebody else in it. Taking her for a ride in the new car would be even better. It would be great—especially today. I had the keys. I'd probably never get them again. If I was able to drive the clunker, I should be able to drive the new car. All I had to do was ease it out of the garage and take it around the yard a couple of times—with Tillie-Jean sitting beside me, saying things like "Wow!" and "Henry, you're really a good driver!" and "I don't know any eleven-year-old boys who can drive a car!" That was what she'd said before. Dad would never know.

"Want to take a little ride in it?" I asked her as calmly as I could.

"In Sweetie Pie?"

"Yep."

"Sure."

"Come on, then."

"Is it okay with your dad?"

"I've got the keys in my pocket."

She gave me another long look but she didn't say anything.

It took us about a minute to get into Sweetie Pie, and we didn't take off our shoes either. I had very carefully watched Dad drive the clunker. That was why I hadn't had much trouble learning to drive it. But there was a big difference between the two cars. And the longer I stared at the instrument panel, the bigger the difference got. Also, the front seat was back too far for me to see over the steering wheel, even though I'm big for an eleven-year-old. I had to look through the wheel. I didn't know how to move the seat forward.

"Anything wrong, Henry?"

"Huh uh."

I finally got the right key in the ignition and turned it. The car started. I put the car in reverse, and it bucked backward and stopped.

"Release the parking brake, please," a voice said—Sweetie Pie's. There wasn't anything she couldn't do! She'd already grabbed us with her seat belts and was cooling us with her automatic weatherized air conditioner. I half expected her to ask if she could do the driving. In fact, right now I kind of wished that she would.

As soon as I remembered where the release was, I did as instructed.

"Thank you," purred Sweetie.

"You're welcome," giggled Tillie-Jean.

At least TJ answered, not the dashboard fax machine. If it had—and TJ hadn't been with me—I think I would have got out of the car right then. But it was too late now.

I started the car again and backed it out of the garage. I surprised myself. With no trouble, I inched it around the backyard, even though the only way I could see ahead was through the steering wheel. I had to sort of pull myself up some to do that. I needed a pillow. I had no trouble going slow because my toe could barely press down on the gas pedal. But every once in a while, when I tried going faster and jabbed the pedal too hard for a second, the car jumped ahead. Tillie-Jean loved that. "Wow! Go faster, Henry!" When I slowed down, she yelled, "Go faster again, Henry!"

So I did. But it wasn't fast enough for her. She wanted more than the backyard too. "Let's go out on the freeway, Henry."

"Not today. Too much traffic."

"Aw, come on, Henry. You're a great driver!"

I nodded. She was right. But I still kept going around and around in the backyard, until she finally said. "Henry, you know what? I think you're afraid to drive out on the freeway."

I shook my head.

"You are too!"

I shook my head but not as much.

"You're scared, Henry Littlefinger!"

"I'm not either."

"You're a wimp!"

The next thing I knew, I was on the freeway going what seemed like a hundred miles an hour in heavy traffic while trying to see through the steering wheel.

I was scared to death. Tillie-Jean was happy as a clam.

2

One way to get old—or dead—very quickly when you're eleven years old is to try to drive a car for the first time on a freeway, especially on a holiday weekend. And when you ought to be sitting on a pillow so you can see over the steering wheel. You also will live longer if you have the front seat close enough to the brake and gas pedals. That way you can put your foot, or at least your toe, on the pedals, especially the brake, without almost sitting on the car floor.

You also should have someone with you who knows how to drive a car and can offer experienced advice, not someone who laughs and claps her hands and yells, "Faster, Henry, faster!"

I wasn't a bit worried about going faster. What worried me was going slower. And I wasn't able to. Somehow I had got into the middle lane of about ten lanes—maybe more—of traffic. Dad had told me that when he was a kid there were only two, three, or four lanes of traffic in each direction, but it sure wasn't that way now. I wanted to slow down and get to the edge of the freeway so I could stop or take the next exit. But every time I tried to do that, a car or truck or bus would get beside me, blocking me. Also, when I started to slow down, the driver in the car behind me would blow the horn, and so I'd speed up again. And when I speeded up, I had to press the gas pedal by sliding down on the seat more. But that made it even harder for me to see ahead because my eye level was lower. All this meant that I was going faster and not seeing as well. Tillie-Jean loved it.

Making everything worse was that I was also too low in the seat to see into the rearview mirror. I wasn't able to see if there was traffic coming up behind me or on my right or left. "TJ!" I yelled, "are there any cars behind me?"

"Lots," she said with a laugh as she glanced out the rear window.

"Help me go to the right!" I cried.

"Turn the wheel, dummy."

"I know that. Tell me when I can turn!" I yelled.

"Why do you want to go to the right?"

"So I can get off the freeway and stop."

"No! Don't stop! Go faster!"

Tillie-Jean had always been a little weird, but I never thought she was nuts.

"You're going to have to help me, TJ."

"You're doing great, Henry. You don't need any help."

A truck horn blasted behind me and to the right just as she said that. I guessed I'd slowed and drifted in front of the truck. The sound made me turn the wheel to the left—too far. As I went to the left, another horn blasted me, this one from the left. So I turned right—too far again. The back end of the car swerved, causing me to turn back to the left—too much again, worse this time. The car fishtailed, and before I knew it we were skidding almost sideways.

Something hit us from the rear, but not hard. In fact, it hit just hard enough and in the right place to help me straighten out the car, but I heard a crash behind us. I wasn't able to look myself, of course. "What happened behind us?" I yelled.

Tillie-Jean surprised me by turning and looking through the car's rear window. The crash must have sobered her some, I thought. "There are a bunch of cars all humped together," she said. "There must have been an accident."

In seconds we were too far away for her to see anything more.

I felt sick. First, Dad's dream car hit. Now I'd caused an accident. I just had to get off the freeway. "Any cars behind us now, or to the right?"

This time she helped me. "Yes," she said, "but not close."

So I started edging to the right, this time doing it very gradually.

I was doing pretty well, I thought, when I heard a siren behind me. I tried to sit up in the seat more to see through the rearview mirror. That didn't work but Tillie-Jean yelled, "A police car is coming!"

I panicked and pushed the gas pedal down. I had caused an accident and the police had seen it and they were after me. If they caught me, Dad would find out not only about the accident but that I'd taken his brand-new car. Then I thought of something worse. Dad had come home early for some reason or other and found his Sweetie Pie gone. He'd thought it had been stolen. He'd called the police. The police car behind us had spotted Dad's car. They thought I was the thief!

I panicked more. I slid down in the seat even farther so I could press harder against the gas pedal. If Dad found out I'd taken his Sweetie Pie, even if I hadn't planned it, he'd kick me out of the house, I bet—if I wasn't already in jail.

With the police car right behind me, I started passing cars and trucks on both sides. Now I must have really been going a hundred miles an hour, but I was afraid to look at the speedometer. I had a lot of close calls, but I was doing okay until suddenly there was a line of slow-moving trucks right in front of us. I couldn't go through them. I couldn't go around them. I couldn't stop. I didn't know how to blow the horn, even if it would have done any good. I didn't even know where the horn button was. I was going to crash into those trucks unless I did something. I jammed on the brakes and jerked the steering wheel to the left at the same time. The car slid sideways for a long time and then finally skidded around into a U-turn and we headed back the way we had just come.

We were now going north against south-bound traffic in the fast lane. On our right was the grassy median strip, but I was too busy to appreciate grass. Cars coming at us swerved away from us in either direction to miss hitting us. I could hear a lot of crashes. I saw one sports car spin around and hit two trucks. I felt sicker. The police car was still behind me. I could hear the siren. Tillie-Jean could see it. She wasn't yelling "Faster!" anymore. I had a hard time getting through and around traffic that was tied up at the spot where I had caused the first bunch of accidents. To get around the stalled cars, I drove across the median into the northbound lanes. Almost at once a taxi sideswiped Sweetie Pie and spun us around so that we were now going south against northbound traffic.

So the same thing started happening to us

again but in the other direction: cars and trucks and buses coming straight at us and swerving in either direction at the last minute. Sweetie Pie's radar screen was going crazy. Some cars crashed into each other and some even went across into the southbound lanes and got messed up there.

I felt even sicker. Much sicker.

Somehow I got into a lane heading down onto an interchange underpass—near Inglewood maybe. I was lost. The police car was still behind us, I thought. Tillie-Jean wasn't saying a word now. She may have had her hands over her eyes. I wished I could have put my hands over *my* eyes. I could hear a siren but I was afraid to look. When I saw a car coming at us up the interchange ramp, I knew we weren't on an exit ramp. We were on an entrance ramp. We were going in the wrong direction again! We missed the oncoming car somehow, and the next thing I knew we were on an East–West freeway under the North–South one we'd been on. Some cars from the North–South freeway above us had skidded down embankments onto the East–West freeway we were now on, as a result of the mess I'd caused up there, I guessed. The skidding cars had caused East–West cars to stop, which in turn caused a backup of traffic in both directions.

Because there was no other place to go, I went into the jammed-in cars as far as I could go, hoping to lose the police car. Tillie-Jean yelled that it was still behind us.

As soon as Sweetie Pie was stopped in the jam, I screamed to Tillie-Jean to get out. We jumped out, I grabbed her arm, and we ran, even though the law says that the driver of a vehicle caught in a traffic jam must stay in or around his car.

And my grandfather tried to tell me you could drive all day when he was a kid without getting into a traffic jam!

3

illustration

T illie Jean and I must have run at least a
mile between stalled, jammed cars and trucks
and buses and vans and motorcycles before we
stopped. I had looked back a few times as we
were running, but I hadn't seen any policeman.
He probably knew he couldn't catch us. If he
couldn't catch us in his police car, how could he
catch us on foot? In spite of everything, I
couldn't help but feel a little proud of myself.

I knew I was going to need all the pride I
could get. I still thought Dad must have come
home and found Sweetie Pie gone and told the
police it was stolen. The best thing for me to do
was to get home and explain everything—or, on
second thought, keep running and come home

in about twenty years and explain everything. For now, though, the only way to get home was to walk. Nothing was moving. Hitchhiking was impossible. The subway still wasn't finished. I climbed up onto the top of an eighteen-wheeler to try to see where we were. Maybe I could see something, like a building, that would help. But all I saw were cars—miles of vehicles on miles of payment.

I groaned as I gazed out in all directions over the jammed-in vehicles. A prairie of them. Which way should we walk to get home? I knew one thing. If we went toward the setting sun, we would eventually come to the Pacific. Once there, we would be able to find our way home because Dad and I live pretty close to the water. Of course, I hoped the jam would end before we had to walk to the ocean. The eleven-month traffic jam of 1999 extended right up to the water, Dad told me. Before it was over, it had trapped cars from San Diego to Santa Barbara and was about eighty miles wide.

Of course, most jams are smaller than that one and last only three or four days. If they last more than twelve hours nowadays, a prefabricated fence is put around the jam. The fence stops motorists from leaving their vehicles and escaping the jam on foot. People are supposed to stay in or near their cars because if they leave them and the jam is broken, the cars with no drivers help cause a new jam. The fence also keeps cars from entering the jam and making it bigger. Helicopters bring food and medicine and doctors and blankets and outhouses and other things that are needed during a long jam. During a real long jam they even bring in ministers or justices of the peace to marry people. They also lift sick people out and women who are about to have babies. Sometimes helicopters even lower big nets over cars in the worst places and lift them out too.

I jumped down from the top of the truck when I saw a police helicopter coming. The police weren't giving up. If they couldn't catch us in a patrol car, they would keep trying in a copter. "Get under the truck, TJ!" I cried. "Police are coming!"

The helicopter went over us as we squirmed under the truck. "Please stay in your vehicles!" somebody in it said through a loudspeaker. "The jam will be broken soon!" The message was repeated as the copter flew on.

"They aren't looking for us," Tillie-Jean said as she came out from under the truck.

"They are too. They're just also telling people to stay in their cars. They're doing both."

I could tell she didn't agree with me when she said, "We ought to borrow somebody's car phone and phone your dad."

"Sure," I said. I was being sarcastic. Just the thought of phoning him gave me the shivers. When I got home, it was going to be tough, face-to-face with him. I sure wouldn't be invisible then. But at least that wouldn't be for a while yet. Tillie-Jean would have the shivers, too, if she'd driven her dad's car without permission and had done to it what I'd done. She didn't know how mad Dad would be when he saw that Sweetie Pie was missing, or how mad he would be when he saw how I had smashed it. If he ever saw it again, that is, in one piece. In some jams, dynamite and bulldozers are used to clear a path through automobiles, and then they are hauled away to a junkyard. I prayed this one wouldn't last long enough for that to happen. I also prayed that the accidents I had caused had not hurt anybody, or at least not hurt anybody bad. If they had, I guess I'd just have to run away. In fact, I just might run away before all this mess was over.

Tillie-Jean did agree with me, though, that the best thing for us to do was to start walking toward the ocean. We both thought we wouldn't be able to find Sweetie Pie. And I thought we shouldn't even try to find it because the police might be waiting for us there—would be waiting there, I thought. From the ocean, we could get home some way. We had no way of knowing if our house would be inside the jam, but I thought it probably was. It had been inside in the past. Cars have been driven right into our yard as drivers tried to get un-jammed. Then the cars got jammed in the yard. We've had guests for days because of traffic jams. Dad kept saying he was going to move to the Midwest where the longest jams lasted only one or two days—so far.

So we started walking toward the Pacific, hoping that when we got there, there wouldn't be any fence. Most vehicles were occupied, but some people had already broken the law and had left their cars, and some cars were not locked. So sometimes it was easier to climb and crawl right through cars than to go around them. Most cars were jammed in bumper to bumper. But some had been spun around. They pointed in all directions. Sometimes this caused spaces in the jam.

It was hot, and we were both thirsty. We managed to get something to drink from one family in a Super-Jamette, an expensive home on wheels. I asked the people in it if they'd heard anything on their TV or radio about a fence being built yet. They said no. They'd only heard a warning being given to motorists outside the jam to stay away from southern California because of the jam.

"Did they say anything about people being hurt in car accidents at the beginning of the jam?" I asked anxiously.

"Yes, they did."

My heart sank.

"They said that no one was seriously hurt in the accidents — just scratches and bruises. They said it was a miracle."

I said so, too, under my breath. What a relief! I guess I wasn't going as fast as I thought I was, plus that today's cars have at least four air bags and are protected by lightweight tank armor manufactured by Mom's Steel, Inc.

We were walking in a westerly direction, of course, and I couldn't help but think of us as sort of pioneers, like the pioneers in the old days who crossed the country to the Pacific Ocean in wagon trains. When I mentioned this to Tillie-Jean, she gave me her special Tillie-Jean Dumb Look.

"Use your imagination," I said. When she kept on with her Dumb Look, I got irritated and said, "Look. You got us in this mess. You were the one who wanted to go for a ride on the freeway."

"Yeah," she said, "and you were the one who was driving. So okay, Mr. Pioneer, get me to the Pacific where I can start a new life."

I decided to shut up about the pioneer life. Besides, I was getting hungry. It was dinnertime. From many vehicles came the smell of food. A lot of people were en route to the beach or someplace with picnic lunches and dinners for the Fourth, I supposed, and now they were eating them in the jam instead. Some had microwaves in their cars, especially the newer vehicles, which also often came equipped with Jam Emergency Kits. These kits had freezers and medicine chests in them. People who had them paid a lower fee for Jam Emergency Insurance. Most people didn't seem too unhappy yet, which was to be expected this early in the jam. Besides, this had happened to most motorists before. They were used to it.

Kids, as usual, were having a ball. It was exciting to them—now, anyway. I don't mean kids my age. I mean very young kids. Older kids didn't want to be penned in any more than adults did. And older kids knew that if the jam lasted a long time, temporary schools would be started inside the jam. These temporary schools were worse than regular schools because there was no room for sports and playing. Healthy kids who were with their families were not lifted out of long jams because the authorities didn't like to separate families. That was why school was held.

One picnicking family gave us each a sandwich and a Pepsi. When Tillie-Jean asked them how far they thought we were from the ocean, a man said about twenty miles. That seemed too far to me. "Why are you kids on your own?" a woman asked. "Aren't you with somebody?"

"Oh, we're just walking around by ourselves for a while," I said quickly. "Let's go," I said to

Tillie-Jean. I started walking. Tillie-Jean followed me. I sure didn't want them to know too
much. I'd seen a phone in their car. I didn't
want them phoning the police to come with
their copters and lift out a couple of poor, starv-
ing kids with no family. And that was what I
told Tillie-Jean as soon as we were away from
the car.

"Maybe you don't want to be lifted out, Mr.
Pioneer," she said, "but I don't mind at all.
Where do you think we're going to sleep
tonight?"

"We're not. We're going to walk to the
ocean."

"Twenty miles?"

"It's not twenty miles. It can't be twenty. "

"Yeah. It can be thirty."

I don't think she even wanted to walk three.
She got that way from her folks, I guess. They
drove everywhere, even if they were going just a
block or so, TJ said. And they were both
healthy. Her dad was a high school coach, in
fact, and her mom belonged to some kind of a
health club. But they were still addicted to cars,
like a lot of people are nowadays. TJ said they
told her that when their folks started to drive,

there weren't any freeways or expressways. When I told her I didn't believe it, she said, "Haven't you ever seen those old movies on TV with cars going along narrow roads?"

"Sure," I said. "They're fakes."

She grinned. "Aw, come on, Henry. You know they're not fakes."

"They're fakes. Like I say, use your imagination."

"If I used my imagination the way you do, Henry Littlefinger, we could fly out of here."

"We can in about a year when Dad says larger cars will be able to tow little helicopters."

"We won't be in this jam a year."

"You sure?"

But Tillie-Jean kept walking with me instead of staying with the family we'd just left and maybe sleeping in their car. It made me feel good.

It was hard walking after it got dark until skyrockets started shooting colored lights over Jamland. The rockets had to be coming from the fireworks at Redondo Beach, which was in the direction we were walking. So I knew we were going the right way. Dad had to be home by now because we were going to watch the fire-

works on TV. And by now he would have discovered his car missing for sure. He would
probably be so upset he wouldn't even know I
was missing too—until he'd decided that I had
taken the car. He knew I didn't like Sweetie
Pie. And with Tillie-Jean gone, too, he'd figure
she was with me in the car.

But all the time I was thinking this, I was
worried about something else. I knew I ought
to phone him. At least TJ didn't have to worry
about that, with her folks in Europe.

After the fireworks ended, a dark silence settled over Jamland. Most everybody, especially
the experienced Jamees, settled in for the night.
Tillie-Jean and I sometimes heard snoring as we
walked along, sort of feeling our way. A half-
moon helped us see some. I was tired. So was
Tillie-Jean. She was yawning, and she hardly
said anything. In fact, she had been quiet for a
long time.

"We have to find someplace to sleep," I finally
said. "Let's look in cars that look empty."

"Okay."

The first time I tried looking in a car a
woman screamed in my ear. The second time I
tried it a man wanted to know who I was. Before

I could try another, TJ found one car empty and unlocked. She got in the back, and I got in the front. I lay curled on the seat a long time, not able to sleep. I knew I should phone and let Dad know we were all right and hadn't been kid-napped or something. But, darn it, it was all his fault. Well, maybe not all. But if he and I had gone to the fireworks instead of his going to that car parts sale, none of this would have happened.

I was finally about to fall asleep when I heard a helicopter coming toward us. I could see it through the sloping windshield. Its searchlight was playing over the cars near us. The light came closer and closer, and the copter seemed to be getting closer to the ground. Then the light was suddenly shining in my face through the slanted windshield. I dropped to the floor. Had the pilot seen me? The copter fluttered over our car for what seemed like minutes, playing the light on it and the surrounding area, as if the pilot was looking for something—us? I could see the light as I lay on my back on the floor. Finally the copter flew away.

Had they seen me through the windshield?

Was Dad in the helicopter?

4

Tillie-Jean and I were awakened at dawn by the sound of another helicopter approaching. It sounded slow and low, as if it was looking for something. I didn't get out of the car we were sleeping in to look for it. I was afraid I'd be seen—or had been seen last night. "Stay inside," I whispered to Tillie-Jean. "Get on the floor." I got down on the floor in the front and she did the same in the back. Lying on the floor looking through the sloping windshield, I was able to see the copter slowly come in over us very low. POLICE was printed on the bottom. Then it moved on, and I couldn't see it. And suddenly I couldn't hear it.

"I think it's landed," I whispered.

"I do too," said Tillie-Jean.

"It had POLICE on it," I said. "They're looking for us."

Tillie-Jean looked puzzled. I was afraid of what she was thinking. Then she said it. "I think we ought to bum a ride out of here on it."

"No! They'll throw us in jail for stealing Sweetie Pie."

I knew I'd said something wrong as soon as I said *stealing*.

There was this long silence. Finally she said, "Stealing it? You mean, your dad hadn't said it was okay for you to drive the car?"

I sighed. "No, he didn't say it was okay."

Silence from the backseat again. "I might have known," she said, "the way you drove it."

"I think I did pretty well, considering the help I got from you."

She snorted. "Well, *I'm* not going to go to jail. *You* stole it."

"I didn't steal it. I just used it without permission."

"Well, whatever. You'll go to jail, not me."

"Okay, me, then."

"So you stay here," she said. "I'll bum a ride out of here."

"No, TJ, no! We're in this together. And you're my girlfriend."

"Girlfriend! I'm only eleven years old, and you're only eight and a half!"

"I'm eleven, too, and you know it!"

"I know why you want me to stay with you."

"You do?" I said.

"Yeah. You want me to be with you when you tell your dad you took his car. Then you want me to tell him that I made you do it."

"You made me drive it on the freeway too," I said, "all the time yelling, 'Faster, Henry, faster!' Don't forget to tell him that too."

Silence. We couldn't see each other because of the back of the front seat.

"Henry Littlefinger," she said, "you're weird."

"Not as weird as you."

She giggled. "I know."

Silence.

"If I stay with you," she said, "can we do something normal after we get out of here?"

"When I'm about forty and out of jail we can."

More silence from the backseat. "Henry," she said after a minute, and I could tell she was going to say something serious. "Your dad would never do anything that would put you in jail, even for a second."

"Oh, yeah?"

"Yeah. You're acting like he loves his car more than you."

"He does."

"That's crazy! He's just weird about Sweetie Pie, that's all. You come first."

"That's what you think."

"That's what I know. You know what your dad told me yesterday before he left? He said, 'I guess you kids would have really liked to go see the fireworks.' He really sounded guilty. 'It's too late to call Joe and cancel out,' he said. 'I sure hope Henry doesn't feel too bad.'"

"He said that?"

"Yes."

"You're sure?"

"I heard him with my own ears."

It made me think. Maybe I was too tough on Dad sometimes, especially lately. Maybe I ought to just let him love his ol' car all he wanted to. Maybe I was just —

Then TJ actually said what I was thinking, and more.

"Henry Littlefinger, don't you realize you're just plain jealous of Sweetie Pie?"

"Well, wouldn't you be?" The words just jumped out. I hadn't thought of being jealous of it—of a car—until just now.

"Maybe. But look. He got that car right after your mom divorced him. He got it to help him get over her. When he talked to it and called it Sweetie Pie, he was thinking of your mom."

"Did he tell you that?"

"No. But don't you think I'm right?"

I shrugged. "Maybe. I'll think about it. How come you know so much anyway?"

Her face came up from behind the seat. She shrugged. "I don't know. Maybe because my mom and I talk about things like that. I talk with my dad too, but more with my mom. About relationships and things. I learn stuff from them." She hesitated, then said, "When my mom was pregnant with my little sister, she and my dad kept talking about the baby coming and what they were going to do for it, buying things and all, going on and on about it, until I got so jealous of it I became a pest, a big stinker.

I was horrible." She was staring at me, hard. "Then Mom had a beautiful baby and everything changed."

A big smile was on her face now. I didn't know what to say, so after a minute I said, "I'm going to try and see where the helicopter landed."

Jealous? Me? All I knew was that it was hard to believe Dad really cared about me when sometimes he didn't seem to know I existed. And why had everything changed after the baby was born? You'd think things would get worse.

I inched my head up from the floor and leaned on the seat until I was peering out the side window. All I could see were cars. I could hear some talking coming from nearby, though, so I carefully eased the door open, got out, then carefully got onto the hood of the car I'd been in and stood up. From the height, I could see that the copter had landed in a small clearing just a few cars away from us. The pilot was talking with some motorists. In a minute, a woman came out of a car with a small child in her arms. She and the child got into the helicopter and it lifted off.

I got back in the car and told Tillie-Jean what

I'd seen. She was still smiling, and when I said, "The kid they carried away was probably sick," a sort of soft look came over her face.

Every once in a while a small open space occurred in a traffic jam, like the one the helicopter just landed in. Sometimes they were caused on purpose by experienced drivers who thought a long jam was coming. They stopped their vehicles with space between them and the cars ahead and maybe to the side. Drivers with cars that could be driven sideways, for parking, were able to do this easier.

The spaces gave people room to do things in—meet there or hang clotheslines or whatever, and kids played in them. The 1999 jam lasted over Thanksgiving Day, which came in the tenth month of the jam. Dinner kits were lowered into the spaces, Dad told me. Each kit contained water and parcels of dehydrated food. When you added the water to each parcel, you got mashed potatoes, peas, turkey, dressing, cranberry sauce, gravy—all the usual Thanksgiving dinner things. Also in the kit was a balloon. When you blew it up, it became a life-size turkey. This was placed on the dinner table to make it seem as if you were having a real turkey dinner. I thought Dad was kidding, but he swore it was true. He said that by the tenth month of the jam, freeway engineers, the police, and the Red Cross were trying anything to help people caught in Jamland, and by then the people caught there were grateful for anything.

Right then, thinking about these spaces, I thought of a way that a jam—any jam—might be broken. Of course, you'd have to make the spaces bigger by pushing vehicles aside. But it could be done. I wondered why it hadn't been tried. Or had it? I decided to think about it some more—along with everything else. Like, maybe if I just yelled into a phone, "Hi, it's me! I'm okay, TJ is okay! We're walking out of the jam! Call the police off!"

5

As soon as the helicopter lifted off, TJ and I started walking westward again toward the ocean. We hadn't gone far when a man in front of another Super-Jamette travel home told us he'd seen on his TV that the jam was a big one and getting bigger. "That means," he said, "that they'll put a fence up both to keep people in and to keep them out."

All I could think was: I had caused it! Me! If they ever caught me, they'd throw me in jail for life! And they *were* going to catch me when I got home—if I got home. Maybe I really ought to run away, disappear forever. Maybe I ought to phone Dad and tell him that—or just never phone him again—ever.

No, I didn't want to do that—not ever talk to Dad. Or see him.

"Used to be," the man went on, "that they'd let everybody out except the drivers, but everybody claimed he was a passenger, not a driver. So now nobody can get out unless you're about to die or something like that."

"Can't people climb over the fence?" Tillie-Jean asked. "Can't drivers break through it with their cars?"

"It would be awfully hard to do either," the man said. "The fence is about a dozen feet high and has barbed wire on the top. And it's made of metal chain links. That's too strong for a car to break through. Besides, guards are all along the outside of the fence—National Guardsmen and police. And sometimes in some places the fence is fixed so that if a person or car touches it, it sends an electrical alarm to the authorities."

"How can they get the fence up so fast?" TJ asked.

"It's kept in rolls at a lot of places in the L.A. area," the man said. "When a long jam happens, thousands of workers put it up in hours."

"It's a wonder people drive cars anymore," I said.

"People are nuts," the man said with a little chuckle. "Like me."

Many more people were walking away from their cars today than yesterday. When I mentioned that to the man, he said it was because they thought the jam would last a long time. "They know it's big," he said. "That's been on TV."

"Did it say if the jam has reached Redondo Beach?" I asked. "That's near where I live."

"Oh, sure. It stretches miles below Redondo Beach. It's nearly all the way to Long Beach." Then he went on to say that more people were also leaving their cars because they hoped to get to the edge of it before the fence was up—and they were hungry too. "Say, have you kids had any breakfast?"

When we said no, he invited us into his home on wheels—it was more like a mansion— showed us where we could wash up, and then fed us a big breakfast of cereal, toast, eggs, and juice. As we ate, he asked us why we weren't with our parents or adults. I answered by asking him if I could use his phone. "Sure," he said.

"I want to call my dad and tell him we're all

right." Then I explained about Tillie-Jean visiting us.

"You go right ahead," the man said. "How did you get in the jam? With some older friends?"

I nodded. I hated to lie, but I was afraid the man had heard on TV or the radio that a kid had been driving the car that started the jam.

"Starting young, eh?" he said, chuckling. "That means you'll spend most of your life in traffic jams. It's hard for me to believe that when my grandmother mentioned jam, the only thing she was talking about was something you spread on a slice of bread."

It was hard for me to believe it too. Maybe his grandmother lived in the middle of a desert.

The man showed me his phone and left me alone. I took a long breath and punched in our number. I was scared. I let it ring a long time, but there was no answer. Dad didn't have an answering machine in the house. He had one in Sweetie Pie, naturally, but it was out now, being repaired under Autocare insurance, which Dad tells me is sort of like Medicare. Today was Saturday. Dad didn't work on Saturdays. He could be anywhere—even at the police station filing a stolen car report. Well, I wasn't going to phone the police, that was for sure!

I was also disappointed. I really wanted to talk to Dad, I know now.

We thanked the man and left. "Drop in anytime," he said with a chuckle.

As soon as we were away from him, I told TJ I hadn't been able to reach Dad.

"If my mom and dad weren't in Europe, I could try phoning them," she said. "I could ask them to keep trying to call your dad. They could do it a lot easier than we can. And I could let them know I was all right in case they somehow had learned I was caught in the jam—with you, I mean. Or I could try calling my aunt in San Francisco—if she had a phone or fax." She grinned. "She's really a rebel. No phone, no fax, not even a car."

Then her grin changed into a dreamy smile. "My little sister is staying with her while my folks are away."

She had mentioned that the day she came to stay with Dad and me. I hadn't paid much attention to it then.

"I can hardly wait to see her," she murmured. "She's so cute and lovable."

Now even her voice sounded dreamy, and I kept waiting for her to say more as she walked along. I wanted to hear more, for some reason. But then a police helicopter darted over us and out of its loudspeaker came: "Please return to your vehicles immediately! It is illegal to leave your vehicle! You cannot get out of the jam on foot! A fence has been put around the jam!"

6

eturn to our vehicle? We couldn't do
that if we wanted to. We wouldn't be able to
find it. And the police might still be there. Or
they might have hauled Sweetie Pie away by
now. And if the fence was up when we reached
the edge of the jam, so what? We could climb it
somehow. Or at least I could, I bet. I began
climbing things when I was wearing diapers. A
dozen feet high was nothing. And I wondered if
a fence would be put up at the ocean. I couldn't
remember if Dad said it was put up there during
the 1999 jam. I asked Tillie-Jean if she knew.
She didn't.

"Why would they build a fence at the
ocean?" I asked her as we walked on. "Where
can you go in the ocean?"

"Hawaii, if you're a good swimmer."

"The Coast Guard wouldn't let you swim anywhere," I said. "They'll have Coast Guard boats at the ocean. Are you good at climbing a fence?"

"I don't know. Do we have to climb it? Your house is inside the jam near the beach, so why don't we walk along the inside of the fence until we come close to it?"

"It would take us forever, TJ, trying to get through all the cars jammed up against the fence. On the outside we can go fast, especially if the fence is against the beach."

We walked on. We weren't alone. More people were now walking toward the edge of the jam, or where they thought an edge was, anyway. They were going in all directions. There was no way of knowing where the closest edge was. I saw a few more open spaces between cars, which made me think more about how they might be used to end a jam if everything else failed. I couldn't help but smile at my idea. I'd keep it a secret until I sprang it on Dad—in or out of jail.

Then right in the middle of the next open

space we came to, who should we see but this cute little kid all by herself, maybe five years old. She was just sitting there, on the freeway, grinning. We couldn't see anybody in any of the cars jammed in around the space.

"She must have wandered off from her folks," I said.

"Yeah. Let's check. We can't leave her here."

We walked up to her. "Hi," TJ said. "Where are your mom and dad?"

She lifted her hand and vaguely pointed off to the right. "There." Then she swung her hand around to the left. "There." Then she giggled.

"Oh," said TJ.

"What's your name?" I asked.

"Stacy. This is Douglas." She nodded to her right.

TJ and I looked at each other. Douglas must be awful little, like invisible.

I tried again. "Are you waiting here for your mom and dad?"

Stacy shook her head. "Say hello to Douglas."

"Hello, Douglas," I said.

"Hi, Douglas," TJ said.

Stacy rewarded us with a big smile. "Douglas is my best friend," she said.

"Great," I said. "But where are your mom and dad?"

"And I'm his best friend," she said. "Isn't that right, Douglas?"

Douglas must have said yes because Stacy gave us an even bigger smile. This kid could really smile.

"Isn't she cute?" said TJ.

TJ was really enjoying herself, and she had the same sort of smile now as she had when she talked about her little sister.

"Yeah, sure," I said. "At least we can help *her*. Look, Stacy, we're worried about you because you're by yourself. Would you like us to help you find your mom and dad?"

She shook her head. "Douglas is with me."

"That's great, but your mom and dad—" TJ began.

"They don't like Douglas," Stacy let her know. For the first time she stopped smiling. "But I do." And she was back to smiling again. "And Douglas likes me."

TJ and I decided to stay with her for a while and hope her folks came back, not that she seemed to need them—or us, for that matter. She never stopped smiling and chattering about her make-believe pal. And when we asked her if she was hungry, she shook her head. "Neither is Douglas," she added. "I just fed him a Big Mac. He doesn't like carrots."

"He *must* be real," TJ said with a grin.

The kid also looked clean—a lot cleaner than us—as if she hadn't been on her own long.

"When did you leave your mom and dad?" I asked her.

"This morning. Daddy didn't like it when Douglas wanted a Big Mac for breakfast."

"So you came here and fed him, right?" TJ asked.

A big grin. "Yeah!"

So there we sat with this kid as she chattered to her invisible pal while people wandered by, thinking we were part of a family, I guessed. As every person crossed the space, I hoped he or she would turn out to be a parent of Stacy. No luck.

"One of us should stay with her while the other one goes looking for her folks," TJ said.

"You mean like walking around yelling 'Hey, Stacy's folks! We've found your kid!'?"

"I guess. You'd think they'd be out yelling for her."

"Maybe they are, but maybe she walked a long way to get here. Maybe they're yelling for her and looking for her a mile or so from here."

"Stacy," said TJ, "how far did you walk to get here?"

"A hunnerd miles. With Douglas."

We were trying to decide what to do when we heard the roar of helicopters coming toward us. Then we saw them. There must have been at least a dozen this time. One by one, they came over us, each giving an order on its loudspeaker: "You must return to your vehicles at once! To leave your vehicle while it is in a traffic jam is illegal! RETURN TO YOUR VEHICLES AT ONCE!"

When I saw the guns, I knew these were not police helicopters. They were military aircraft, with guns protruding out of the front, rear, and bottom. Dad had told me that when jams got too large for the police or the highway patrol to handle, the National Guard was called in. They weren't flying over us one by one just to give us orders. They were flying over us to show us their guns. Each gun pointed downward.

"Are they going to shoot us?" Tillie-Jean cried.

"Get under a car!" I yelled.

I grabbed Stacy and we scrambled under the nearest vehicle. It luckily turned out to be a truck loaded with concrete blocks. No bullets could go through the blocks.

We lay there until all the copters had flown over us, their guns staying silent. Then, as I peeked out and up, they flew outward about two hundred yards or so and regrouped. And then in a great circle they flew around the area where we were hidden—we and dozens more, maybe a hundred.

We waited for the guns to start firing.

They never did. After flying around us for a few minutes, the copters all flew off except one. It dropped something. A small parachute opened. Dangling under it was a small pouch. It floated down toward us. It landed near the truck we were under. I was the first to reach it, and I opened the pouch. Inside was a hunk of smooth metal, for weight, and an envelope. Inside the envelope was a letter. People crowded around. A man tried to take the letter out of my hands, but I wouldn't let him have it until I read it out loud.

"To: All People Confined in the Current Traffic Jam. You are hereby warned that those who depart their vehicles are violating the laws of the State of California. If you do not return to your vehicles, you will be prosecuted to the full extent of the law.

"You are being observed. Return to your vehicles at once or be prepared to accept the consequences.

Very truly yours,

Kaspel Twid

Kaspel Twid, Commander
California National Guard"

The man who'd grabbed for the letter was carrying a rifle. He was young, and his eyes looked wild. As soon as I'd finished reading, he cussed, raised the rifle, aimed it at the distant helicopter, but didn't fire. "Get out of here!" he bawled. "If you want to enforce the law, get the subway finished!"

People reacted differently. Some became very quiet, some said, "No, not that," or words like that. Some, though, cheered. And some laughed when one woman said, "Maybe he's a caterer and all his caviar has gone bad."

When everybody had either read the letter or heard what it said, somebody yelled out, "I say we wait here until evening, then head for the Pacific in the dark! We should make it by dawn!"

Somebody else yelled, "Right! Who do they think they are? This is the USA!"

Others yelled the same sort of thing, and a great cheer went up. Somebody yelled, "Tomorrow the Pacific!"

Or the fence, I thought.

Stacy cheered too. She was standing between TJ and me, enjoying the show. I supposed Douglas was too. He was probably even cheering.

All of a sudden Tillie-Jean grabbed Stacy under the arms and lifted her up so she was sitting on TJ's shoulders. Then as soon as the cheering stopped TJ yelled at all the people grouped around, "Does anybody know Stacy's folks? Here she is! She's lost!"

She didn't have to yell it more than twice before a man ran up, looking relieved and happy. He reminded me of how my dad used to look—happy, I mean.

7

Stacy yelled, "Daddy!" as the man ran up. As he reached out for her, TJ bent over so that Stacy fell into his arms. He said, "Stacy, darling baby," as he hugged and kissed her. "I've been looking all over for you, where have you been?"

"Here," she said, "with Douglas."

The man looked at TJ and me. Tears were in his eyes. "Where did you find her?"

"Right here, not long ago," TJ said.

I nodded. I really felt good, best I'd felt since I'd been in the jam. So did TJ, I could tell. And she seemed older.

"She was just sitting in this space, all by herself," TJ told him.

"Oh, thank you, thank you so much." He wiped his tears. "After breakfast," he said, "she told me she was going to take a nap with Douglas in the back of our van." He sort of grinned and groaned at the same time. "She does a lot of things with Douglas any time of the day. I didn't know she was missing until the helicopter dropped the pouch. I went to get her, to come out here, and discovered she was gone."

The man had never stopped hugging Stacy as he talked. It made me feel even better.

"My name is Ty," he said. We told him ours. "You kids want some lunch?"

"Oh, we're not hungry," I said.

"I'm hungry," TJ said.

"Come on to my van then," Ty said, "and I'll make you a sandwich."

"All right," TJ said, and off they went through the jammed cars. So I went too, beginning to worry. Next thing you know he'd be asking us all kinds of questions.

Ty's van wasn't too far from the open space, and it wasn't nearly as big as the home on wheels where we'd had breakfast. Ty made all of us sandwiches of various kinds of lunch meat, except for Douglas. He had an invisible Big

Mac, and of course we had to make a place for him at the little table.

"Now, tell me about yourself," Ty said as we were eating. "You aren't lost too, are you?"

"Nah," I said. "We're okay." I was hoping that would satisfy him, but it didn't.

"You're alone?"

I liked that question, though. This guy seemed to think it might just be possible that a couple of kids could be in a jam on their own.

So before I knew what I was saying, I said, "Sure. We don't live too far from here." I grinned. "This is our backyard."

"It's not mine," TJ let him know. "I don't live in L.A."

'She's visiting me and my dad."

"You need any help?" Ty said.

"Nah," I said.

"You're welcome to stay in the van as long as you like." He was looking at TJ. Then he looked at me.

She hesitated, then shook her head as she bit into her sandwich.

"We're walking out of here tonight," I said. "Are you?"

He nodded no. "I'll sweat it out here in

the van. It will be better for Stacy, I think."

"And Douglas," Stacy added.

"And Douglas," said Ty. "You want to stay in the van until you leave?"

"Sure," I said.

"Great," said TJ. "I could stand a nap."

"You have a phone?" I'd been thinking about it even before we got to the van.

"Sorry, no."

Then, for some reason, I wanted to ask him if he had a wife. I guess it was because I'd been wondering ever since we met him where his wife was, or if he had one. I mean, like my dad, he had a kid and was alone. I wondered if Dad would cry if he thought I was lost—seriously lost. Cry when he found me, I mean.

But I didn't have to ask him.

"I wish I had a phone," he said, "so I could phone my wife."

So did I.

8

As soon as it was dark we said good-bye to Ty, Stacy, and Douglas, and started out. There must have been twenty-five or thirty of us, fewer than there had been earlier. I guessed some had got scared and changed their minds.

The nut with the rifle was still with us, muttering that he was sick and tired of waiting for the Los Angeles subway to be finished: "I moved to L.A. years ago so I could ride the subway—I love subways—and I haven't even seen a part of it opened. An inch! All I do is get jammed! I was on my way out of town on a hunting trip a couple of days ago when, sure enough, it happened again!"

People didn't know whether to laugh at him

or keep their distance. One thing for sure was that he was turning into a pest.

Walking was hard. It was an overcast night. Only a little moonlight helped us see. Everybody had to use his hands to keep from bumping into cars. The good thing about it, for us, was that it was so dark nobody could tell we were by ourselves. Sometimes I took TJ's hand and led her. Sometimes she took mine. A man with a compass and a shaded flashlight was leading. I hoped he knew where he was going.

Everybody stayed quiet. It was safer. The only time we talked was when people in cars asked us where we were going, or what was going on. We told them in whispers. Some joined us. I was afraid our group would get too big. It would be dangerous because we might make too much noise and attract the attention of the helicopters. We could see the lights of an occasional copter in the distance. We whispered to newcomers not to use lights and not to talk.

A baby near us started to cry, and the woman carrying her couldn't make her stop. Right away TJ began to talk soothingly to the kid, trying to get her to shut up. TJ was having only a little luck until she wiggled her nose in the kid's belly and made a blowing sound. The kid shut right up and began to smile.

"Good going, TJ," I whispered. She was handling this kid even better than she handled Stacy.

She grinned. "I've had a lot of practice." I could tell she was proud of herself.

"With your little sister?"

She nodded.

I wondered how I'd do with a little sister if she began to cry and wouldn't stop. Or with a little brother. I had an idea I wouldn't be good at it.

"You must have really practiced a lot," I said.

She nodded again, then gave me a long look. "It takes a lot, especially if you're jealous at first. It takes a lot of practice just to get over that."

It made me think.

"Do you think I could get over it?"

"Sure, if you tried hard enough."

I was thinking about that when a woman suddenly cried out to a man she was with, "Harry, I'm afraid!"

"Shh," he said.

"I'm afraid. I don't want to do this."

"Be quiet!" he told her. He was mad.

Three or four people whispered loudly for them to shut up. They dropped out of the group, and it was quiet again. Very quiet.

But even though it was quiet, I felt as if I was communicating with everybody in our group, not just thinking about Dad. It was funny. Nobody was talking but we were still communicating. We were close. . . . I really wanted to get home now and explain everything . . . talk. We hadn't talked much since Mom left. Maybe I could do the same thing TJ did with her folks—talk. And stop being jealous. I didn't have a baby sister to practice on but . . . Well, there was you-know-who. She must be right about Sweetie Pie being a substitute for Mom. Look what he named it!

More and more now we could see the lights of helicopters in the distance. Most had their searchlights aimed downward. "We must be getting close to the beach," TJ whispered.

"Yeah," I whispered back.

I felt her hand tighten on mine.

Suddenly a copter shot toward us. It happened so quickly we barely had time to dart under or inside empty vehicles. Its light was aimed down. Searching for us? I wondered. It swooped right over us, without seeing us, I hoped.

The jerk with the rifle muttered something as the copter disappeared in the distance. Tillie-Jean and I edged away from him. He scared us—subway or no subway.

Finally, we began to hear the surf. Then, in the first light of day, we saw it. The fence. We crept closer. It was at least a dozen feet high, with barbed wire along the top. It had been put up right against the sides of cars and other vehicles, right where the freeway ran alongside the beach. We could see the ocean through the chain links. Some people began to wonder out loud if they could climb it. Others agreed that it kept people out of the jam.

We were all disappointed. We'd hoped there would be no fence at the beach.

"What do they expect cars to do," one man said angrily, "drive into the jam from the sand!"

"Maybe they've put the fence up here to stop boats from sailing into the jam," a woman said sarcastically.

"Or swimmers from swimming into it," TJ said. "Or fish."

Then I saw something that made me whisper excitedly to Tillie-Jean. "I know where we are. I can see the end of a pier to the left that Dad and I have fished off. In the distance, see it?" I thought for a moment. "We're about seven or eight miles from home." I looked up and down the beach some more. "And I don't see any soldiers or policemen. If we can get over the fence, we'll be free."

Everybody else must have been thinking the same thing because about half of the group began to work an automobile back and forth, moving it toward the fence. I was afraid that the fence might be fixed electrically so that it would set off an alarm when it was touched, and I whispered a warning. "We'll just have to take that chance," one man answered.

When the side of the car touched the fence, there was no alarm that we could hear. But I worried that an alarm had been set off at National Guard or police headquarters.

Our plan was to climb on top of the car and then go over the top of the fence. But when early risers in nearby cars saw what we were doing, they called out for us to stop. They said police and soldiers were on the beach. They said we would be seen if we tried to climb the fence. We'd be caught.

We gathered around one man and woman who got out of their car. "Yesterday three people that I know of tried to climb the fence," the woman said. "Not one made it. One man got caught in the barbed wire, and a police helicopter saw him and reported him. Soldiers came and got him. The other two got over the fence, but soldiers saw them and caught them on the beach."

"If any of you are thinking of climbing over it," the man said, "you better wait until dark."

We decided that was what we'd do. Some of us decided to do that, that is. Some changed their minds about climbing the fence, especially after a National Guard helicopter landed on the beach. About ten soldiers got out of it and began to patrol in front of us.

Another helicopter suddenly swooped in low over us, its loudspeaker screaming, "Return to your vehicles at once or suffer the consequences! You are in extreme danger!"

"Look!" Tillie-Jean yelled.

She was pointing at the subway man. He had his rifle aimed at the helicopter. He was only a few feet from me, so I ran to him, grabbed the rifle barrel, jerked it down, and held it down with both hands. He cussed and tried to yank it out of my hands, but I hung on as he bawled, "Let go!"

Two men ran up and grabbed him and the rifle, and I let go. Other people began talking to him, trying to calm him, but he kept staring at me. Finally, he yelled, "I would have shot him down if it hadn't been for you! Stay away from me!" It made me shiver. I was glad when a woman took me by the arm and led me toward a Greyhound bus.

TJ followed me inside. "Are you all right?"

I nodded.

She gave me one of her long looks. "Are you sure? That was so scary."

I kept nodding.

"I think we ought to sleep in here today," she said.

I thought that was a good idea. When we woke up, we'd try to climb the fence as soon as it was dark.

It took me a long time to go to sleep. I sure was glad we were inside the bus.

9

It was still light when I woke up. I was too excited to wait inside until it got dark enough to climb the fence. I looked out the windows on both sides of the bus for the jerk with the rifle. I didn't see him. I hoped he'd left the area, or at least calmed down. But mainly I hoped somebody had taken his rifle away from him.

I went to the fence. I couldn't see any soldiers or police on the beach, so I went back to the bus, woke up Tillie-Jean, and asked her if she wanted to climb now. She gave me a big yawn and tried to go back to sleep, but some people offered us food and she got up. After we ate, we went out to the fence. I wanted us to be the first to go over it. The sooner we put some distance

65

between us and the subway addict the better I'd feel.

People who were going to climb the fence were ready to do it. They were mainly young people. About a dozen of them. Most older people said it was too dangerous, even some who had walked to the fence with us. They'd changed their minds.

We weren't the first in line to go over the fence. A man who had brought a pair of wire cutters from his truck was first. He got on the roof of the car we'd pushed up against the fence. The rest of us lined up behind him. But when Tillie-Jean and I tried to get into the line, some jerk said, "You kids can't go over that fence. It's too dangerous." Right away everybody else said the same thing. "You kids get back in the bus," a woman said. "I'll bring you some soup."

"Soup!" I cried. "We've come here to climb, not eat! What do you mean, we can't climb the fence! We've been walking for days to climb it!"

"Besides, we've just eaten!" TJ let her know.

"Right!" I said.

"And we both hate soup!" she yelled. "We like danger!"

"We're going to major in it in college!" I screamed.

"Where are your parents?" somebody else wanted to know.

"Waiting for us on the other side of the fence," TJ bawled, "crying for us, biting their nails, tearing out their hair!"

She went a little too far with that one. We heard laughs.

We argued, we yelled, we screamed, but we didn't make any headway. Not one adult agreed with us.

Finally I said to Tillie-Jean, "Let's get out of here!" And down alongside the fence we marched. We'd find our own place to go over it. Too young! Who did they think they were talking to? Somebody who couldn't drive a car?

We left just in time.

We hadn't gone much more than a hundred yards or so when searchlights from boats right off shore flooded the area we'd just left. The Coast Guard must have sent in boats in the darkness. At the same time the lights went on, we saw headlights moving rapidly on the beach from both directions. They were heading for the spot where our group was climbing the fence. As we looked back, we could see the lights focus on one climber at the top of the fence and others below him. Two helicopters had also roared in over the area, and their searchlights were also on the climbers, who all changed their minds and dropped back on the inside of the jam.

"Somebody must have warned the police," Tillie-Jean whispered.

I nodded. "Somebody who was already in the area we got to this morning, I bet."

"Somebody who was afraid there would be trouble."

I kept nodding. "Yeah, especially after our funny pal tried to shoot at the helicopter. But now it's going to make it better for us. The police and National Guard will think they've stopped the escape attempt. Right?"

"Maybe."

"So now is our chance to go over the fence," I said. "They'll shut off the light and go back to where they came from."

"I hope so," TJ said.

She didn't sound too enthusiastic.

Then all of a sudden we heard a yell, then yells coming from near the fence where we'd just been. Then somebody shouted, "Get him before he gets us all killed! Get that rifle away from him!"

When I heard that, my heart sank. That crazy nut was on the loose. He still had his rifle. And he was mad at me. Suppose they chased him our way. Or suppose he just ran in our direction.

Then, sure enough, the yelling seemed to be getting closer. I could see flashlight beams aimed toward us.

"Quick, TJ," I whispered. "Hide! They're chasing that crazy man toward us!"

I grabbed her arm and pulled her into the back of an empty car beside us. We crouched down in the back as the yelling got even closer. We held on to each other. I could feel her trembling. I was too. More lights were flashing in the sky. I hoped the police and National Guard were looking for the weirdo too. I hoped they would come inside the jam and catch him.

I wished we were a couple of Douglases ourselves right now—invisible.

Gradually the yelling and cries stopped and the lights faded away. I guessed everybody was going back to where they'd started. But we hadn't heard any big yell or anything to show they'd caught the man.

Finally I whispered to TJ, "We have to find a car close to the fence so we can get on top of it. Then we'll be high enough to climb over the fence."

I couldn't see her, but I knew she was giving me one of her long looks—an extra long one. "I can hardly wait," she said.

We got out of the car and started creeping along the fence, and I started worrying about something else. If we stood on just an ordinary car would we be tall enough to reach the top of the fence and climb over it, especially with barbed wire on top? The barbed wire itself worried me too. I'd never climbed over any, and I didn't even bother to ask Tillie-Jean if she had.

We crept along, keeping close to the fence. Luck was with us. It didn't take long for us to come upon a van with its rear end right up against the fence. And not only that. When I quietly climbed up on top of the van, I found an erect, opened-up stepladder on top of it. A wide board extended from the top of the ladder, over the top of the fence, and right over the barbed wire. People in the van must have escaped that way. They must have had the ladder inside. I thought maybe the owner was a carpenter or something like that.

Tillie-Jean agreed with me, especially after we found out the van was empty.

"I hope they got away," she said.

I nodded. "But we have to be careful. If they were caught on the beach, the police and soldiers might be waiting for somebody else to try it right here."

"But the police would have taken the board down."

"Maybe they haven't seen it yet. Maybe the board was just put up tonight and the people escaped just a little while ago. But we still have to be careful."

"Right. You first, Henry."

Then I thought of something worse. Suppose the man with the rifle had not been caught and had put the board up.

10

██████████████████████████

I couldn't see any lights or hear any sounds on the beach, so I started inching out over the board on my hands and knees. The board angled up, but it wasn't too steep. Tillie-Jean waited on top of the van—to see if the board broke, I figured. I wasn't worried about that. It felt strong. It was tricky when I got to the end of the board, but I made it over the barbed wire and dropped to the beach.

Then it was Tillie-Jean's turn. She zipped over the board and dropped down beside me. "Let's go," she said. And we did.

Keeping close to the fence, which was on our left, we headed south, walking fast and quietly—but not too fast. I didn't want to catch up to the frustrated subway rider or step on him. Just the thought of that petrified me. Weird as he was, he might just decide to sleep on the beach. It was still partially cloudy and foggy, and so there wasn't much moonlight. If the pier I'd seen was the one Dad and I fished off, we were on Manhattan Beach. If I was right, we were about two miles north of where Artesia Boulevard hits Hermosa Beach. And if we kept going about two or three more miles on the beach past Artesia, we'd hit Torrance Boulevard. Then we'd turn left onto Torrance for about three miles and we'd be in our neighborhood.

When we got closer to the pier, I knew it was the one I thought it was. It was a new pier. And when we got even closer we could see a soldier on guard duty under some lights. We stopped. The soldier was walking back and forth in front of the pier. "When his back is toward us," I whispered, "we'll get up and run. But as soon as he turns around and starts walking toward us, we'll stop and fall to the ground until he turns around and starts back."

"Okay."

We did it the way I suggested, and we got by him. The subway man could have too.

We went on. It was late by now, and we were hearing some snoring on the other side of the fence. And every once in a while someone would say hi—or wouldn't say anything if he thought we were soldiers or the police, I thought.

When we got to Artesia Boulevard, there were more lights and more guards.

"How are we going to get by here?" Tillie-Jean wanted to know.

"Swim," I said.

She stared at me. "I didn't bring my swimsuit."

"Who cares? I didn't bring mine either. We can swim in our clothes. We'll get them clean."

"I've never gone swimming in my clothes," she said. "I'm afraid I'll drown. They can stay dirty."

I thought for a moment. I sure didn't want a drowning on my conscience too, "Okay, we'll wade," I said. "You can wade with your clothes on, can't you?"

"I don't know. I've never waded with my clothes on either."

"There's nothing to it," I said. "All you do is walk in water."

In southern California even in July the ocean wasn't what you'd call hot, especially at night. But gradually we got used to the cold. We waded out until the water was up to our chins, then turned left and slowly went by the lighted area with no guard seeing us. Then we came back to the beach and fence.

Then Tillie-Jean began to sneeze. She couldn't stop. She woke up people sleeping inside cars just inside the fence. They yelled at us. I guessed they thought we were guards.

"Walk faster!" I whispered. "That will warm you up and maybe you'll stop sneezing." There was now enough light behind us to let us see ahead a little ways—to stop if we saw the weird man.

We began to walk faster, but TJ kept sneezing. As far as the soldiers were concerned, they couldn't hear the sneezing. But as we got close to Torrance Boulevard, I could see they were also on guard there, and the area was lighted. I knew we'd never get by the boulevard without the soldiers hearing us. If we tried to go around the area by wading in the ocean, her sneezing would probably be even louder because she'd be colder and wetter.

She agreed with me after I told her all that.

I thought about everything for a minute. "So what we'll do," I said, "is go back inside the jam."

She stared at me as if I'd gone completely boffo. "Go back inside the jam?"

"Sure. Inside, it won't make any difference if the soldiers hear you sneezing. Besides that, now I'm positive our house is on the inside. It's near Torrance Boulevard, and as you can see, Torrance is inside the jam. That means the house has to be inside too. All we have to do is find Torrance on the inside of the jam, turn left on it, keep walking, and we'll be home!"

"With cars all over everything, how will we know it's Torrance Boulevard when we find it? And how will we stay on Torrance if we find it?"

"That's what is worrying me," I said.

"We can read the signs, can't we? The road signs?"

"Once we get away from the fence we can't. They turn the lights off on the signs during a long jam to make it harder for people to walk out of the jam. But we'll be able to know when we get to Torrance because lights will be on near the fence."

"*Ah-choo!*" she sneezed. "Oh."

"But I don't know what else to do but try," I said. "Do you?"

"No. But I wish you'd thought of going back inside the jam before I got wet. How are we going to climb back over the fence?"

"Good question. If there was a pile of sand next to the fence, we could climb up it and then go over the top."

"Sure. And if there was an elevator next to it, we could even do it easier."

"If we had a balloon, you could sneeze in it and we'd float over."

"Very funny. *Ah-choo!* I'm going to stick my nose in the sand."

"That's it!" I whispered excitedly. "We'll dig under the fence if we can find a place where the fence is over the beach a little instead of over the freeway."

"We won't find any place like that unless the people putting up the fence got drunk or something. *Ah-choo!* If the fence was over the beach, people inside could dig right under it."

"Well, let's look, anyway."

"It's no—*ah-choo!*—use."

We were afraid to get any closer to the lighted area at Torrance Boulevard. So we turned around and started back along the fence the way we'd come. We walked real close to the fence, putting our feet down right next to it. This way we were walking right on the edge of the freeway, because the fence posts were in the pavement. We couldn't see much, but if we stepped on some beach, we'd know it, and could maybe dig there.

I knew Tillie-Jean was behind me because of her sneezes. They came more often now and were louder than ever.

That was why I actually wasn't too surprised when the subway nut suddenly appeared in the dark ahead of us and aimed his rifle at me. "Freeze!" he said in an angry whisper. "I know who you are, you little shrimp!"

I froze, all right. And so did Tillie-Jean.

"If it hadn't been for you, I would have downed that helicopter with one good shot," he whispered. "A shot that would have been heard around the world. A shot for freedom from traffic jams. A shot for a subway!"

"Yes, sir."

"Don't you realize that you represent a generation that will have to lead Los Angeles out of the wilderness of traffic jams into the glory of a subway?"

"Yes, sir."

"I bet you have never even been on a subway."

"No, sir."

His voice changed. It became soft and dreamy. He lowered his rifle. "Oh, what a thrill lies ahead for you. What excitement. What joy. What happiness as you zip here and zip there."

TJ never had stopped sneezing, and right then came a thunderous *AH-CHOO!*

That was why I wasn't too surprised a second time. As the subway man jerked his rifle up at the sound of TJ's sneeze, a shot came from behind us, and the rifle went flying onto the beach near us. With an angry yell, the man ran to pick it up. I dived for his legs, grabbed one, and hung on as he dragged me toward the gun. But when TJ grabbed his other leg, he fell to the beach short of the rifle.

Then two soldiers with rifles ran up and grabbed him. And two police officers grabbed us.

11

So we who had been trying to get *out* of the jam were caught trying to get *in* it. If everything hadn't been so scary, I might have laughed at that, but as the soldiers took the weird guy away, I couldn't even smile.

Neither could Tillie-Jean. All she did was keep sneezing. One of the first things one police officer did was pull a handkerchief out of her pocket and offer it to Tillie-Jean.

TJ thanked her and went *ah-choo* again.

"Do you need a handkerchief too?" the other police officer asked me.

"No thanks," I said. "All I need—we need—is to get back inside the jam so we can go home. We live in it."

I then explained everything to them, except for one thing—I didn't say I had been driving a car. All I told them was that we had been in my dad's car.

"No problem," said one of the officers. "I'll call a helicopter to come get you and take you two home."

"Great!" I said. "But I thought helicopters wouldn't pick up anybody unless it was an emergency." I was a little bit suspicious and afraid. Even though I hadn't given them my name, did they somehow know I was the kid who had taken his dad's car and started the jam?

"This is an emergency," one officer explained. "You kids are out in the middle of the night. Your dad must be worried sick about you. How did you get separated from him? Is he home or in the car?"

"Oh, we just wandered away," I said vaguely. "He's at home, I guess."

"That's illegal," the officer said. "He should have stayed in the car."

I was afraid she was going to ask me Dad's name so she could report him, but she didn't.

Then I got worried all over again when TJ

asked her, "What happens to people who don't stay in their car?"

"They're fined."

"That's all?" I said. I was really surprised.

The officer nodded.

"What happens to people who are caught trying to climb over the fence?" TJ wanted to know.

"They're fined."

"That's all?" I was even more surprised.

So was TJ. "Nobody gets locked up?"

Another nod. "Just fined."

I couldn't believe it. I wish I'd known that before.

"It used to be," the officer said, "that people were put in jail for breaking jam laws, but the city had to keep building jails to hold everybody, so they just fine lawbreakers now."

The officer used her walkie-talkie to call a helicopter, and it wasn't long before it landed on the beach near us. The pilot opened a window and said with a grin, "Guess what, you kids. That rifle that man had didn't have a bullet in it."

TJ and I just stared at each other. I sure wished I'd known that too.

The officer told the pilot where we wanted to go. We thanked the officers and got inside. I had never been in a helicopter before, and I was excited, but also still nervous. I wouldn't be able to relax completely until we were home. Tillie-Jean was excited too, and didn't seem even a little nervous. She quit sneezing right away and cried, "I hope he goes fast!"

He did, flying close to the ground. Tillie-Jean was once again happy as a clam. Why does everybody think clams are happy? If I were a clam, I wouldn't be a bit happy.

The pilot was able to follow Torrance Boulevard because he had a special map of the area for helicopter pilots. It was on a television screen. As the helicopter flew over an area, the screen automatically changed and showed the pilot that area and where he was on it. A searchlight was also on the bottom of the helicopter to help the pilot see.

So it didn't seem to take hardly any time for us to get home. The trouble was that when we got there, the searchlight showed that our yard was packed solid with jammed-in cars. Everybody's yard was. There was a little space in the yard, but it wasn't large enough for a helicopter to land in. And it wasn't large enough to be used in connection with my idea of how to end jams, I thought. Of course, with my idea, even a space large enough for a helicopter to land in would have to be made bigger by shoving cars to the side.

The pilot lowered the helicopter until we were only about ten feet off the ground. Then he kicked out a rope ladder. The upper end was tied down inside the copter. "Good luck," he said as we started down.

We got down okay. The pilot pulled the ladder up and flew away.

I didn't know what time it was, but it must have been about 3 or 4 A.M. Our house was dark. We walked between cars and then between people sleeping on the front porch. I knocked on the door. Pretty soon a light came on inside and Dad yelled, "Who's there?"

"Henry and TJ!" I yelled back.

As soon as Dad heard me, he unlocked the door and just about jerked us inside and started hugging us. "Good Lord, where have you two been? I've been worried sick. I've phoned the police and the National Guard and the hospitals and the Red Cross and anybody else I could think of. I didn't phone your mother in Europe, though, TJ. I didn't want to worry her. But I was going to if you didn't show up. Where have you been?"

I told him the whole story—everything, except the part about how I felt about Sweetie Pie. There wasn't any need to mention that, I thought, even though my feelings had a lot to do with my driving the car. Besides, my feelings had changed now.

But Dad wanted to know about that part too. "Why did you take the car, Henry?" he said when I'd finished. His voice was soft.

"Because TJ wanted me to," I said.

"I thought you had permission!" she cried. "You had the keys in your pocket. It was my idea to go on the freeway, though," she admitted.

Dad put his hand on her arm. "It's okay, TJ." Then he said to me, "Why did you do it even if she wanted you to?"

"Because I wanted to, too."

"That bad?"

"You'd never let me drive it." I began to get mad. "You'd hardly let me get in it. 'You might get Sweetie Pie dirty,' you said. Things like

that. You worried about your car more than
. . ." I stopped.

"You?" Dad asked gently.

I didn't say anything, but Dad knew. He
hugged me even harder. "Darn it, Henry,
you're more important than any car. Can you
understand that?"

I nodded. TJ was nodding too.

"Do you want me to get rid of it?"

"Well, you sort of have," I said. "It's kind of
wrecked."

We were staring at each other—hard. He was
really seeing me now. I could tell. I wasn't any
invisible Douglas, that was for sure.

I swallowed and said, "Maybe we can fix it."

I saw tears in his eyes.

"Maybe," he said.

"We can try," I said. "I can help find it."

"I can too," TJ said.

I really felt like helping. It made me think of
TJ's wanting to help with her kid sister after she
stopped feeling jealous. Maybe I wasn't jealous
anymore either. It felt good.

I waited a moment, then said. "Did you
report it stolen?"

"No. I thought you'd taken it for a ride with

TJ and would bring it back. That police car was probably chasing you because of the accidents. It was a miracle nobody was hurt."

"So I guess the helicopters weren't after us either," I said.

"No."

I was feeling a lot better, but there was still one important thing bothering me: I had started the jam. Tillie-Jean had talked me into driving on the freeway, but I didn't have to do it. I was responsible for causing thousands of people a lot of trouble. And that was what I told Dad.

"That's why we're going to go talk to the police tomorrow," he said.

I slept late. When I woke up and looked out the window and saw the little space in our yard, I thought once more about my idea to end traffic jams. I also noticed that in the distance cars were beginning to move.

At the breakfast table Dad told us he'd just heard over the radio that the jam was beginning to break.

"In that case," I said, "my idea about how to end a real long jam won't have to be used—this time."

"What's your idea?" Dad asked.

"All you have to do," I said, "is to make the spaces you see in jams big enough to build an interchange ramp in each space."

Both Dad and Tillie-Jean looked at me suspiciously.

"So?" Dad said.

"The ramp would lead to a new freeway," I said.

"A new one?" Dad said.

"Sure. One that wasn't jammed. One that had been built after the jam started."

"Where?" Dad asked.

"Where else?" I cried with a grin. "Right on top of the old one!"

And that was one of the things I told the judge when I had to go to court. I don't know if it helped, but he grinned and let me off with a warning.

Sweetie Pie? We kept it. We use it more now. Dad got the dents knocked out of it. There were plenty, believe me. But he doesn't wash and polish it the way he used to. He does the driving.

We both talk, though.

When TJ visits and rides with us she never

asks Dad to go faster. She's happy just to get where we're going. One freeway jam is enough for her. She never asks me to drive her either — not even in the yard.

That's fine with me. I don't have much of an urge to anymore.

About the Author

John Keefauver was born in Washington, D.C., and was graduated from the University of Maryland. Since then he has worked as a circus press agent, a substitute teacher, and a newspaper reporter, among other things. His freelance writings have appeared in numerous publications, including *The New York Times*, *Omni*, *The Christian Science Monitor*, and *Playboy*. He has contributed to many short-story anthologies.

Mr. Keefauver has traveled extensively in the South Seas, Central America, Asia, Europe, and the Yukon. He lives in Carmel, California, where he enjoys walking on the beach and driving fast on curvy roads. He hates traffic jams.